Who Visits Me from  to

An Alphabetical Adventure To the Dentist

Written by Joanne Roos, RDH

Illustrated by Maggie O'Keefe

Published in United States by CreateSpace

ISBN:1502573873

ISBN-13:978-1502573872

For Melissa,
my brightest smile

A is for Alligator.
Do you think an Alligator is Allowed at the dentist?

Absolutely not!!
Alligators don't know how to take care of their teeth.

Do you know how to take care of your teeth?

What kind of animal is this?
It has two Big Buck teeth.
I Believe it's a Beaver!

Do you think a Beaver Belongs at the dentist?
No way! Beavers are too Busy.

Where does a Beaver live?
Beavers live By the water.
They use their BUCK teeth for Building dams.
Beavers can't Behave at the dentist.

C is for Crocodile.
Can a Crocodile get his teeth Cleaned and Checked at the dentist?
Certainly not!

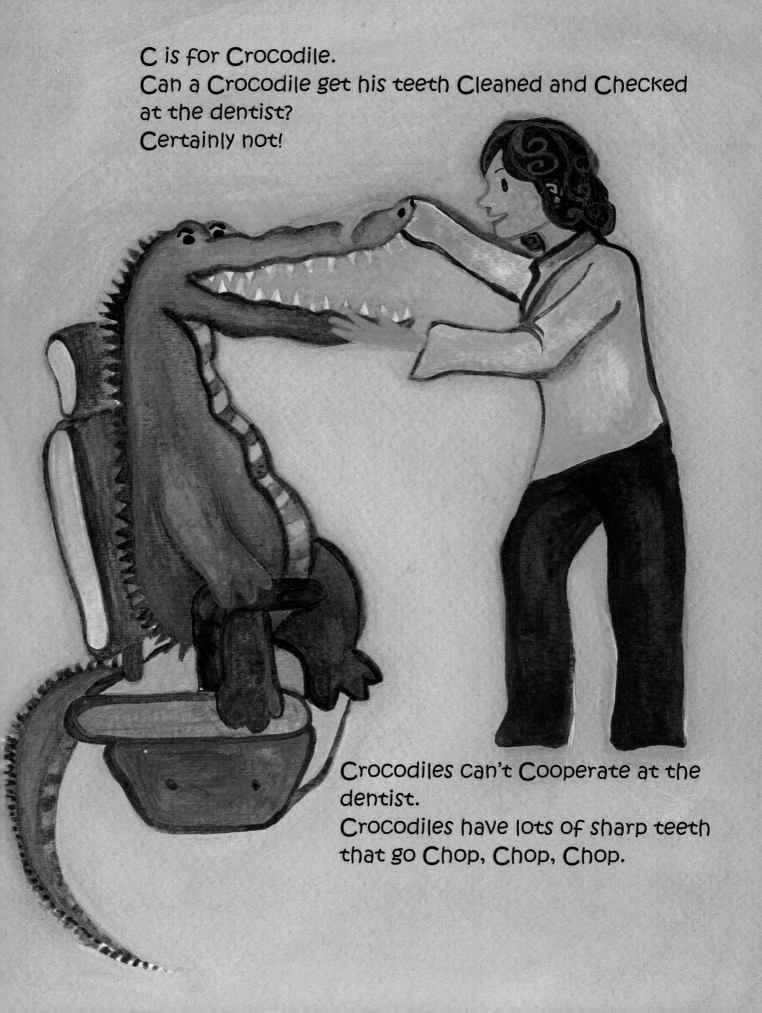

Crocodiles can't Cooperate at the dentist.
Crocodiles have lots of sharp teeth that go Chop, Chop, Chop.

Where does a Crocodile live?
A Crocodile lives Close to a swamp or by a river.

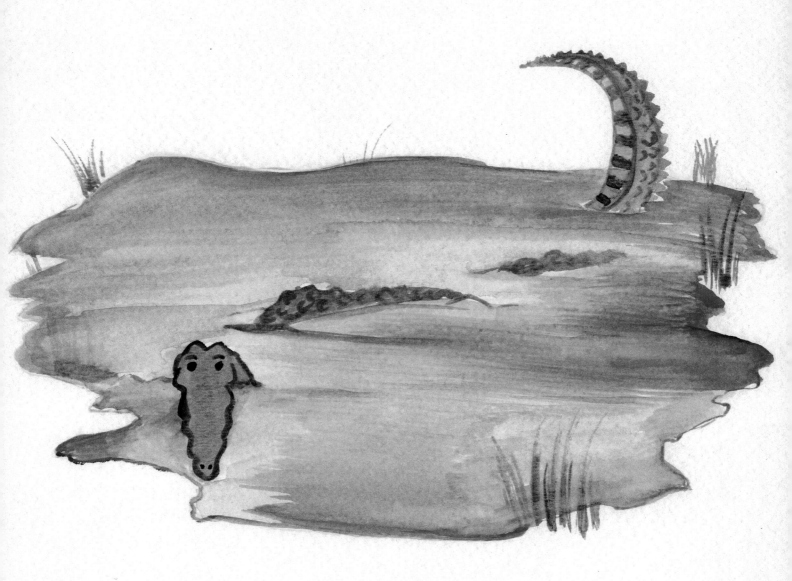

I don't want a Crocodile to Come and visit me at the dentist!
They're dangerous!

Do you know what kind of animal goes quack, quack, quack?
It's a Duck!
Do you think a Duck goes to the Dentist?
Definitely not!

What would a Duck Do at the Dentist? Ducks Don't have teeth!

Where does a Duck live?
Ducks live Down by a lake and
Dive in and out of the water.

Who is this?
It's an Elephant!

Can an Elephant Enter the dentist's office?
Never Ever!
Everyone knows Elephants are Enormous.
Elephants can't fit in the dentist's Chair!

Where does an Elephant live?
Elephants live in Africa,
Asia and Even at the circus.

F is for Fox.
Can a Fox Find the dentist?

I don't think so...

Where does a Fox live?
Foxes like to run and hide in the Forest.
Can you Find the Five Foxes hiding in the Forest?

Do you know what kind of animal this is?
It's a Giraffe.
Can a Giraffe Go to the dentist?
Gosh no!
A Giraffe Grows too tall to Get into the dentist's chair.

Where does a Giraffe live?
Giraffes live in Africa.
Do you know that Giraffes are the tallest animals on earth?

Have you ever seen this animal?
He is a Horse!
Can a Horse go the dentist?
I Hope not!

Horses have more teeth than Humans and chew on Hay all day long.

Where does a Horse live?
Horses like to run free or live on a farm.
Sometimes an animal doctor checks a Horse's teeth to make sure they're Healthy.

What kind of animal do you think this is?
It's an Iguana!
Can an Iguana get Into the
dentist's office?

Impossible!
Iguanas are Incredible lizards and
have tiny sharp teeth.

Where does an Iguana live?
Iguanas live near oceans and In trees.
I don't want to look Inside an Iguana's mouth.

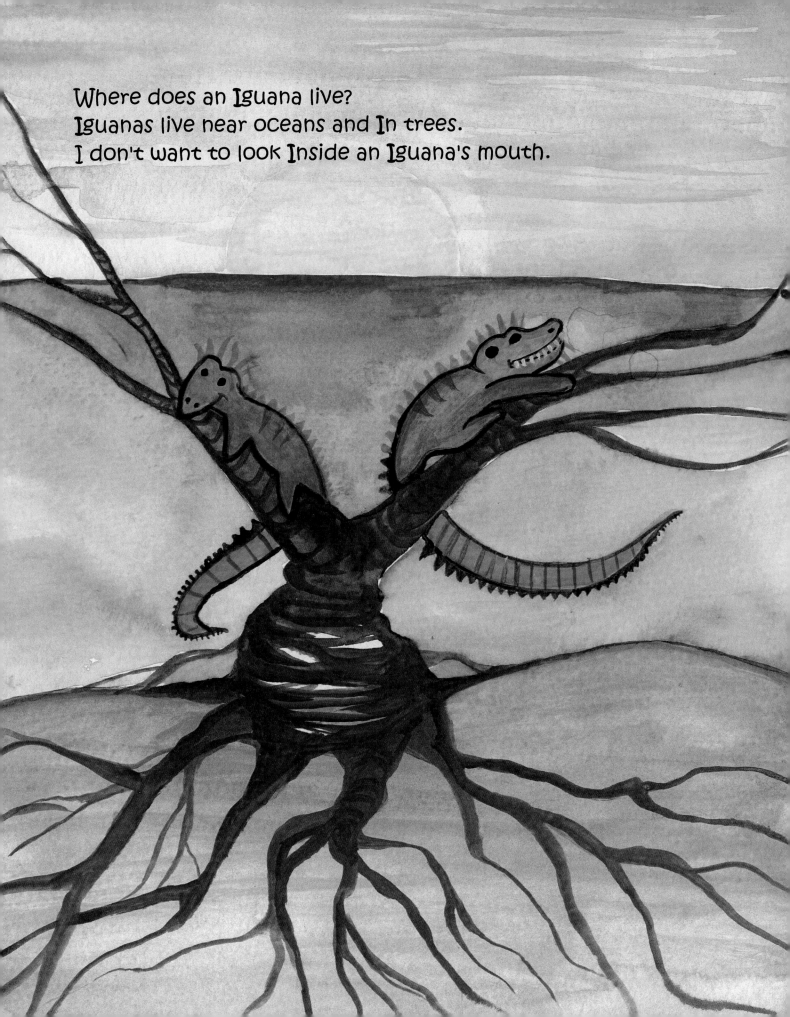

What kind of animals are here?
They are a Jaguar, her Kitty
and a Lion.
They are Jungle cats.

Can Jungle cats Just show up at the dentist?
You must be Joking! They have very big Jaws and Jump around too
much!

Where do Jungle cats live?
They Keep hidden in the wild or Live at the zoo.
I don't want a Jaguar or any Kind of Lion
to visit me at the dentist.
What Kind of sound does a Lion make?

Maybe you know who this is?
This is a Monkey!
Do you think a Monkey can Make it to the dentist?
Most likely not! Monkeys are cute but they Mess around too
Much.

Where does a Monkey live?
Most Monkeys live in the rain forest, or the jungle.
Monkeys Make a lot of noise.
What kind of sound does a Monkey Make?

What kind of animal do you think this is?
This is a Numbat.
Numbats are anteaters.
Can a Numbat go to the dentist?
NO, NO, NO!

Numbats Never go to the dentist.
They don't have proper teeth.

Where does a Numbat live?
Numbats only live in Australia.
They have a long Nose and a very long tongue.

Do you have a tongue?
Always remember to brush it!
Can you find the Nine ants the Numbat is looking for?

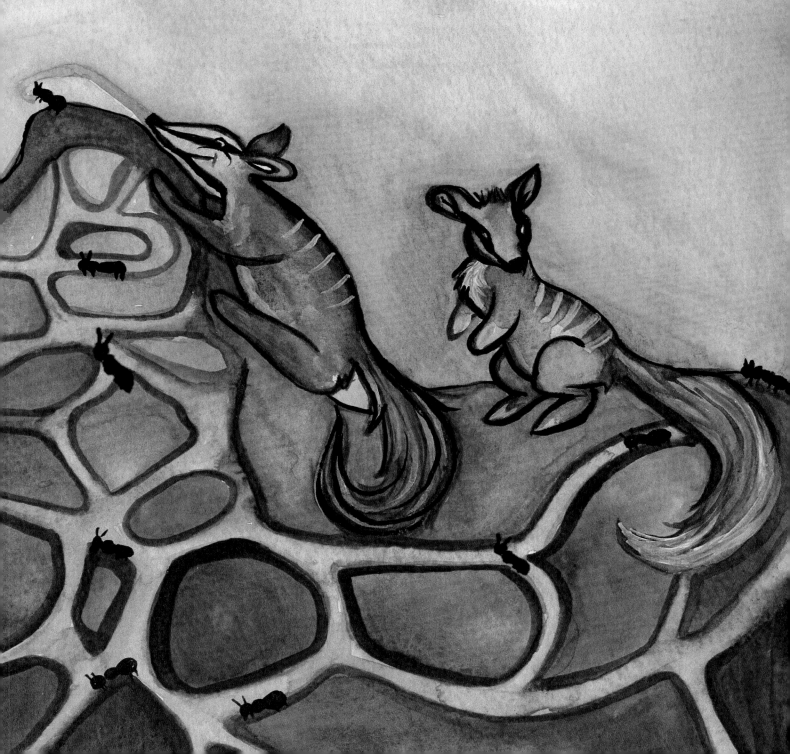

What do you think this looks like?
It's an Octopus!
Can an Octopus visit the dentist?

Oh no!

An Octopus can't swim

up to the dentist!

Where does an Octopus live?
They live On the bottom of the Ocean.
Do you know that an Octopus has teeth On its tongue?

P is for People.
Can a Person like a girl or boy Pay a visit to the dentist?
Positively yes!
Do you think you can Pay a visit to the dentist?

People need to visit the dentist to get their teeth cleaned and polished to prevent cavities.
Big People can go the dentist, and little people can go to the dentist, too!

These are my friends Quinn, Roger and Sam.
They are little kids with baby teeth.

They love to visit the
dentist.
When they are done
they can
Quickly
Reach into the
treasure chest
for being a good
listener.
Can you be a good
listener like Sam?

This is Tracy, Ursula and Veronica.
They are big kids.
They know what's going to happen
at the dentist's office.

Tracy takes her Time To
brush before her visit.

Ursula will Use
a special brush
because she has
braces.

Veronica just
finished her checkup.
She has a Very Very nice smile.
Do you have a nice smile?

Waiting at the dentist are Wanda and Xavier.
They are Tracy's mom and dad.
Can mommies and daddies go to the dentist?
They sure can!
Wanda Will be next and Xavier is
getting an X-ray.

This is grandma Yana and grandpa Zack.
Do you think grandmas and grandpas can go to the dentist, too?
Yes, Yes, Yes! Grandparents love to visit the dentist and they
Zoom in and out with clean white teeth.

Next time they come
you can come too,
this is what the Dental Hygienist
will do.

I count them and check them
and tickle your teeth clean,
I get front teeth and back teeth
and even in-between.

I paint them with fluoride
to keep them strong,
so your grownup teeth
last all life long!

I show you how to brush
in the morning and night,
so your teeth can stay
healthy, shiny and bright!

Now that your cleaning and checkup is through,
you see how easy it is to do.
So come any time to visit me,
it's as easy as
going from A Z to !

Happy Teeth

Brush in the morning
and brush at night
keep your teeth clean shiny and white
scrub front and back
and use a soft brush
do inside and outside
there's no need to rush
brush up and down for two minutes long
so teeth can stay bright healthy and strong
please don't forget if you're old or young
you always need to brush your tongue
follow these steps and in a short while
you'll have great teeth and a beautiful smile

What's To Eat - A Snack Or a Treat?

When you're looking for something good to eat
know the difference between a snack and treat
snacks can be fruit, veggies or cheese
you can eat these snacks whenever you please
treats have more sugar
just have one or two
and lots of sweet drinks are not healthy for you
eat right and keep fit
go to recess and gym
healthy choices are smart
to keep active and trim

Dear Parent/Teacher:

Introducing young children to the dentist at an early age helps develop healthy life-long oral care habits.

Preparing them for that first dental visit is essential to make it a success.

This book will not only show your child what to expect but also create excitement and an understanding of what happens during a dental visit. It is intended to gently encourage children and help build a positive attitude for future visits.

The American Academy of Pediatric Dentistry recommends that your child visit the dentist around his or her first birthday. Follow up visits should occur once or twice a year.

Remember.....it is never too early to start taking care of your child's teeth!

Joanne Ross

Made in the USA
Middletown, DE
22 March 2017